THE LOST DOVE

THE LOST DOVE

A STORY FOR ALL TIME

ELIANE WILSON

Illustrated by Hans Erni

ELEMENT

Shaftesbury, Dorset • Boston, Massachusetts
Melbourne, Victoria

© Element Books 1998
Text © Eliane Wilson 1998
Illustrations © Hans Erni 1998

First published in Great Britain in 1998 by
Element Books Limited
Shaftesbury, Dorset SP7 8BP

Published in the USA in 1998 by
Element Books, Inc.
160 North Washington Street, Boston MA 02114

Published in Australia in 1998 by
Element Books
and distributed by Penguin Australia Limited
487 Maroondah Highway, Ringwood, Victoria 3134

The moral right of the author has been asserted.

Cover illustration by Hans Erni
Cover design by Mark Slader
Design and typesetting by Mark Slader
Typeset in Adobe Caslon
Printed and bound in the Great Britain by Butler and Tanner Ltd,
Frome and London

British Library Cataloguing in Publication
data available

Library of Congress Cataloging in Publication data
Wilson, Eliane.
   The lost dove : a story for all time / Eliane Wilson : illustrated
by Hans Erni.
      p.   cm.
   ISBN 1-86204-311-6 (hardcover : alk. paper)
   I. Title.
PR6073. I4635L6   1998
823'.914--dc21   98-22913
                                                  CIP

ISBN 1-86204-311-6

Some day, after we have mastered the winds, the waves, the tides and gravity... we shall harness the energies of love. Then for the second time in the history of the world, man will have discovered fire.

Teilhard de Chardin

To the memory of *Père* Bruno Hussar.
Also to my father and mother, who told me stories.

CONTENTS

THE VILLAGE WITH THE GREEN SHUTTERS

*It is not wisdom to be only wise
and on the inner vision close the
eyes. But it is wisdom to believe
the heart.*

Santayana

*I*t was early morning in the Pays de Vaud, a land whose earth is blessed by the gift of corn, wine and salt. Embraced by the terraced vineyards, the village had just woken, shaking off its mantle of snow silently fallen during the night. In the village there were houses with green shutters, a church, a school and a manor house whose living stone changed colour with each passing hour, each passing season.

Stefan was walking alongside his grandfather. The old man was a printer, as his father had been, and the father of his father before him. They were craftsmen–poets who printed with the timeless beauty of classical alphabets, designing pages of harmonious simplicity to set the words. They lived and worked in communion with the mountains which enfolded their land of fields and vineyards, streams and forests.

In time of storms the mountains shrouded themselves in angry greyness, and clouds galloped furiously like wild-maned horses. But as the sombre cloak suddenly tore apart, it revealed the white snow summits, always there, reaching to the skies. Then the drifting clouds would stretch into wings of haze (perhaps to entice the absent angels), and Stefan wanted to cling to them in the search for his dove. But that was to happen later . . .

For Stefan his grandfather's workshop was an enchanted world, coloured by the iridescence of the inks and permeated with the smell of the leather used by his grandfather to bind the printed sheets. An old oaken bookcase stood in a corner, the books on its shelves filled with magical illustrations of faraway lands, and with the wisdom of their ancient traditions. But the object of wonder for Stefan was a very large book in which his grandfather often wrote. 'It is our Family Chronicle,' he told the child as he turned the sepia-stained pages on which hands now long silent had written of their everyday lives, confided their dreams, and lovingly recopied passages from writings which had inspired them. One day, Stefan would fill the still empty pages with a magical tale.

On one of the earliest pages, Stefan's great-great-grandfather had transcribed the Craftsman's Prayer, which would inspire the work of his sons, and of the sons of their sons.

THE CRAFTSMAN'S PRAYER

Help me at the outset of the work, where I am most weak; help me in the heart of the task to hold taut the thread of attention, and above all, may you, yourself, make good the deficiencies of my work.

Lord, let there be in all the work of my hands, some of your grace to speak to others, and some of my imperfections to speak to myself. Keep me in the hope of perfection, without which I should lose heart. Keep it beyond my power to achieve perfection, without which I should fall victim to pride. Purify my looking, for when I work badly it is not certain that it is bad, and when I work well, it is not certain that it is good.

❧

Lord, let me never forget that all knowledge is vain save when there is work. And that all work is empty; save when there is love. And that all love is barren which does not bind me to myself, and to others, and to you.

❧

Lord, teach me to pray with my hands, my arms, and all my strength.

❧

Remind me that the work of my hands belongs to you, and that it behoves me to surrender it to you when parting with it. That if I work from a desire for gain, I shall decay in the Autumn like an ungathered fruit. That if I work to please others, I shall fade in the evening like the flower of the grass. But if I work for the love of the good, I shall remain in the good. And the time to work well, and to your glory, is now.

Amen

To teach Stefan to read, his grandfather gave him some paper and helped him to print out letters with the wooden characters of an old printing press. His grandfather told him stories, and read him poetry. It did not matter that Stefan couldn't understand it all. The sound of the words was enough then – the understanding would come later; when Stefan would touch, see, hear, and recognize his own being in the poet's vision, when he would see his own life and dreams, but always linked by a constant love to memories of a childhood rich in warmth, protection and happiness.

Once, when he was still a very young child, his grandfather had opened the family Bible and read to him the story of Noah.

And the waters of the flood were upon the earth ... And the rain was upon the earth for forty days and forty nights ... And God remembered Noah and every living thing and all the cattle that was with him in the ark and God made a wind to pass over the earth and the waters assuaged ... and Noah opened the window of the ark he had made and sent forth a dove; but the dove found no rest for the sole of her foot and she returned unto him into the ark. And he stayed yet another seven days and sent forth the dove out of the ark; and the dove came in to him in the evening and in her mouth was an olive leaf ... and he

*stayed yet another seven days; and sent forth
the dove; which returned not again unto him
any more ...*

The next day, the old craftsman engraved a Dove of
Peace on a piece of pear-tree wood. Stefan placed her
above his desk in the workshop and the dove became
the child's constant companion and confidante,
to whom he told of his joys and sorrows. Together
they listened to the stories and tales recounted by
Stefan's grandfather and, one day, Stefan took her to
the pear tree in the orchard. Holding the engraving
tightly under his arm, he climbed to the tree-house
his father had made for him, and he showed the
dove the branch from which she had been carved.

Stefan and his grandfather had just passed the
church. Christmas was fast approaching and pure
notes of music escaped through the narrow windows
into the crisp, bracing air of that December morning,
mixing with the smell of new bread which came

from the Grande Rue each time the door of the bakery opened. Above the roofs of the village, the smoke was drawing blue arabesques, while the weathered tiles, dusted with snow, were slowly warming under the hushed, wintry sun. It was an ordinary day like any other day; but as he entered the workshop, Stefan stopped, spellbound. His eyes grew wide. The wood-engraving was hanging on the wall above his desk, where it had always been, seemingly untouched, against a background of forests and mountains, but the dove had disappeared.

Stefan searched for her in every corner of the workshop – behind the printing press, among the inks and the sheets of paper, on the shelves of the oaken bookcase – but nowhere was the dove to be seen. And that day, around the world, doves flew out of paintings, broke out of stained-glass windows, and kicked off their pedestals of stone. They broke away from mosaics, tore away from tapestries, and stole out of manuscripts. In years to come, people would speak of that day as the day – and here their voices would lower to a whisper – when the doves flew away. They deserted man, to whom they had given their purity of heart, their perception of sight and their love of light, and the olive groves were left bereft.

And gone was the dove which had flown through the pages of the Bible, from the Book of Genesis to the Prophets and the Song of Songs; the dove, symbol of the Divine Spirit, which had inspired the sacred writers and sat next to Saint Gregory as he composed the sublime chant; the dove which had rested on the shoulder of the Prophet Muhammad as he conversed with the Angel Gabriel.

And from the tales of wisdom spun out in ancient lands – the Orient and the land of turquoise and roses; the land of ancient seers and the land of prayer wheels; the land of icons and silver birches, and the lands of the Slav – the doves flew away. They flew from the land of tall grass prairies and bison; from the Stone-Age land of rock-painting and honey-guides; from the land of Ossian the Gaelic bard, the fair isle of saints, scholars and singing birds; and from the land of Prometheus, home of the Muses.

And gone was the dove which had been held tight by the trusting hands of a child, drawn by the painter of Guernica; and the dove which had listened amidst the Umbrian hills to a man in sandals and a brown robe who spoke of Peace and reconciliation.

Stefan knew well the story of Saint Francis of Assisi, the troubadour of God who loved nature and spoke with all creatures. Perhaps, Stefan thought, he too could learn the language of the birds and find out what had happened to the doves. And because birds can feel the innocence and the purity of a child's heart, they taught Stefan their language. In the orchard, each day at dawn, at the hour when their song in celebration of the light invites man to listen and see with his heart, they taught the child their language. The language, some say, which Adam spoke when he named the animals filing past him one by one in the Garden of Eden, a very long time ago.

And like illuminated pages unfolding in a Book of Hours, the march of the seasons went by, healing in their unfailing renewal. In the village there was joy and pain, new life and passing away, and the trees added one more ring to the inner core of their wood, and one more, and another . . . and Stefan was no longer a child. But still at dawn each day he spoke with the birds in their language, and still he waited, waited for his dove to return.

She returned one morning to the village with the green shutters. There was a scar on her breast. She told Stefan of a quest, of faraway lands, and of a Council of Doves held in an olive grove where it had all begun.

II

THE COUNCIL
OF DOVES

Je t'ai filé une chanson douce
Comme un murmure de colombe
à midi…
Je t'ai tissé une chanson et tu ne
m'as pas entendu.

L.S. Senghor

*T*here was no time to say goodbye, explained Stefan's dove. The call had been urgent. It said: 'Fly to the Mount of Olives without delay. The Council of Doves has been convened.' She had left the wood-engraving and the village with the green shutters, and flown towards Lac Léman. On the shore of the lake, outside a house dedicated to the Olympic Spirit, stood a Greek statue. Opening her hand of bronze, she let go a dove of white marble which flew towards Stefan's dove as she passed her by. Soon after, a dove which had deserted the pages of an ancient Irish Chronicle joined their flight, accompanied by a dove painted by Braque, which had deserted the Etruscan Ceiling in the Louvre Museum.

They rested in a mimosa grove that night, on the shore of the Mediterranean Sea. Waiting for them there was a dove from Assisi, flown out of a fresco painted by Giotto; and a dove which had abandoned one of Chagall's biblical gouaches.

At dawn the next day, guided by a dove sent from Jerusalem to lead them to the Mount of Olives, they flew together towards the Land of the Bible. One day they would fly back to the mimosa grove to tell each other of their quest. But this they did not yet know . . .

As the doves came to rest in the olive grove on the Mount of Olives, each one received a leaf. Etched on the silver grey, in chilling starkness, was the number of wars in our era. Then the wise and ancient dove who had convened the Council spoke to the birds: 'Our ancestor, the Second Dove, brought back to Noah an olive leaf plucked from this grove.

Of the Third Dove, although Noah waited for her day after day, he never heard again, nor did mankind. But then one day a Storyteller, hunted down by men of hate, and his books burned to ashes – *and strange to say his name was Stefan too* – would reveal her story. The story of the Third Dove, "who had flown forth into the infinity of space, from darkness into light, and in an ecstasy of vision floated across the world; who had forgotten Noah and her mission, forgotten she must return, and nestled in the green shade of a wood as the years passed her by."'

In the grove on the Mount of Olives, there was silence. Even the silver leaves had ceased rustling as the wise and ancient dove repeated the words of Stefan Zweig, the Storyteller.

'"One day the whole wood began to roar and crack as though the very world were falling apart. Black masses of metal screamed through the air and where they fell the earth leapt in horror and the trees were snapped like grasses. Men hurled death at one another and fearful machines spewed forth fire and flame . . . The Dove awakened from her dream. Death was all about her, and destruction . . . She fluttered upwards and flew across our world in search of Peace, but go where she would she found everywhere the same man-made lightning, the same man-made thunder, everywhere was war . . . Quickly she flew across the land, searching for a place of rest whence she might return to the patriarch bearing the olive leaf of promise in her bill . . . She has not yet found a resting place, nor humanity Peace, and until then she may not return home, she may not be for ever still.

"'No man has seen her, the lost and mystical Dove in her search for Peace, but still she flutters over our heads, frightened and with pinions that are already weary. Sometimes, deep in the night, a man awakening from a startled sleep may hear wings beating high in the air, haste in darkness, anguished, unheeding flight. Upon her is the weight of all our sombre thoughts, in her fear are carried all our wishes, and there fluttering between heaven and earth is the Lost Dove . . . And once again, as those thousands of years ago, the world is waiting, waiting that a hand be put forth to take her, waiting for the knowledge that the trial has been at last enough."'

In the grove the wise and ancient dove paused. The doves' hearts were beating wildly, their chests heaving with anguish. Then she spoke again: 'I have summoned you to entrust you with a mission. Go and find the Lost Dove, the Dove of Peace. Help her in her search for Peace. Then, but only then, can you return to your homes.'

'But where shall we find her?' Stefan's dove asked. 'How can one bird alone . . . ?'

'The road to Peace will not be easy,' answered the wise and ancient dove. 'You will often travel on a road veiled in bitterness and yet all of you will journey to lands where peace, goodness and blessing, life, grace, loving kindness and mercy are waiting, longing to be rediscovered. These gifts you will bring back to man to help him in his search for the Lost Dove, the Dove of Peace.'

Then she turned to Stefan's dove and said, 'You will fly to a faraway land in your search for the Lost Dove, but you will also be our messenger to man so that our quest becomes his quest, our journey his journey.'

Clouds rose above the Mount of Olives, clouds of silver-blue wings over Jerusalem brushed the harp of David, the shepherd anointed King, who each dawn sings his psalms in praise of the Creator. And to the four corners of the earth the doves flew away, to search for the Lost Dove, the Dove of Peace.

In the village with the green shutters that morning, Stefan opened the Family Chronicle. Turning the pages, he recognized the handwriting of his grandfather, the craftsman poet, who had passed away one summer afternoon while Stefan held his hand. The skies were as blue as cornflowers, and the cemetery, when they had laid Stefan's grandfather to rest, looked like a garden, edged by orchards on one side and by fields of maize on the other; and from the church nearby the sound of the bells reminded the dead they were still part of the village.

'Yesterday,' Stefan's grandfather had written, 'the buds in the orchard unfolded a promise. Today in my arms, I held my grandson Stefan, born with the morning and the pear trees in blossom, taking part in the joy of a child's new life.'

Stefan continued reading; I shall take you by the hand, my grandson, to rediscover together, without haste, the mystery and the wonder of the beauty around us; to drink her colours, listen to her music. And long after I cease holding your hand, may you keep new, fresh and pure, the innocence and the limpid clarity of childhood; its joys a source of strength all throughout your life.'/

Now it was Stefan's turn to write in the Chronicle. As the dove began the tale, he took up the pen to recount on the white page the doves' journey in their search for the Lost Dove, the Dove of Peace.

A DOVE PAINTED BY
CHAGALL WHICH FLEW
TO AFRICA

Afrique… comme un coeur de réserve.

Aimé Césaire

'Come with us!' the white storks flying over the Land of the Bible had called to the dove which had left Marc Chagall's gouache to fly to the Council. And the dove had followed them on their way to Africa. Her heart was singing. Had not Chagall said whilst he painted her that 'in life all is possible when conceived in love, that/it is our duty to colour our own lives with shades of love and hope'?/

To Africa she had flown; to her many lands where man, rooted in the ancestral memory, is at one with nature and with the unseen. There on the M'Gandi fig tree, in the shade of which the elders once sat to

29

speak of Peace, sat the Bundi; but the old and wise owl had not seen the Lost Dove, the Dove of Peace.

Over parched burning sands and over the Land of Ophir, whose gold was sent to Jerusalem to build King Solomon's Temple, the dove flew, and on over the ancient Kingdom of Cush, towards the Land of Sine. In that ancient land she asked the *dyâli* – the troubadours playing the *kôra* – if they had seen the Lost Dove, but the strings of their harps kept silent. Then, in the breathing of the African night, the drum rose, asking the dead and the living, the wind and the stars, if they had seen the Dove of Peace? They had not, and with the dawn, in a sob, the drum felt silent. So on and on Chagall's dove flew, until she had reached the land of the honey-guide, the small brown-olive bird which leads man to honey.

As the dove was resting on a sycamore branch, it came and perched next to her. 'Have you seen the Lost Dove, the Dove of Peace?' she asked.

Fanning its tail with markings of white, the honey-guide spoke: 'First came Dxui,' it said. 'The First Spirit of Creation, whose works were many. He gave things their names, and was present in each of his creations. The First Spirit of Creation – says the Bushman who runs like the wind – was flower, tree, fruit, water, bird, and man. When other men rejected and hunted him he became tears, the tears of the rejected and of the hunted; then he became flower again, but a flower with thorns, because he had been rejected and his loneliness was great.'

Night had fallen in the land of the honey-guide. There was music and dancing round the fire. The women were singing, clapping their hands. The men were pounding the red earth with their naked feet, and while they danced, they recreated the spirit of the forests, the animals, the moon and the stars. And the earth was responding, her rhythm rising, enfolding their whole being, giving them strength.

'To show the sweetness of his love for all his

Creation,' the honey-guide continued, 'the First Spirit painted the animals, the birds and their eggs with different colours, and fixed them with honey. He then made me the honey-guide, the bird of thorn-apple trees, kinder-hearted than a chief, *tswedi tswerre*, the bird which leads men to honey. So men followed my song, until we reached the hollow tree in which the bees had stored the amber honeycomb, and to reward me, the whistling bird of the bees, they shared some of the honey with me.

'I led men to honey,' it explained, 'honey, the symbol of wisdom which the wise men of Africa sitting under the M'Gumu tree in council had safeguarded and transmitted down the ages. Then their peoples were as one. And when they met, they would greet each other, recognizing beyond the tribal and the kinship ties a shared humanity, their diversity bound by the mortar of solidarity. Then man was a family.'

Now the morning star had come to sit with

the dove and the honey-guide. At the water hole, the shy antelope and the magical springbok were drinking, together with the other animals that man had carved and painted on the golden sandstone. The honey-guide then began to sing, inviting man to follow the song which leads to honey. From branch to branch it flitted, its song becoming more and more insistent.

But from Africa's many lands of red earth and of sunset's splendour, man no longer a family was fleeing man, and no one came to follow the song of the honey-guide. Under the M'Gumu tree (in which dwells the spirit of all the forests' felled trees), there was silence only; their palate no longer made sweet by the honey, the elders and the wise men of Africa no longer sat in council to transmit the wisdom of the past. But still the honey-guide sang.

The honey-guide gave the dove some honey to take back to man, to remove bitterness and bring delight

to his heart. The dove, whose wings now were honey-gold, left for the journey home. But first she flew to the mimosa grove to tell her tale, enfolded by the elusive blue of hope . . .

In the Family Chronicle, Stefan wrote a verse by Tagore which his grandfather had read to him when he was still a child: *Faith is the bird that feels the light and sings when the dawn is still dark.*

In the village with the green shutters it was spring, 'the time of the singing of the birds'. (But was it perhaps their singing which made spring blossom into being?) The trees were drinking deep from the soil, and in the fields and the vineyards, men and women, stewards of the land who shared her heartbeat, were working and toiling.

At the windows, the eiderdowns, having borrowed the colours of the lilac and the wisteria, greeted each other in the morning air as Stefan's dove continued the tale . . .

CHAPTER

IV

A DOVE CARVED IN WHITE
MARBLE WHICH FLEW TO
HELLAS, THE ANCIENT
LAND OF GREECE

*I was not born to share hate
I was born to share love.*
Sophocles

They called her Hellas. In this land, we are told, sculptors fashioned images not from living models, but from the ideal beauty they saw with the inward eye alone; and the columns they tore out of the marble and threw to the light were an offering to the gods of the cosmos, which in their language meant the universe, its order and beauty. It was then that the dove of white marble was carved. In another time, she would fly from the shore of Lac Léman where she had made her home, to the Council of Doves, and there, on the Mount of Olives, she would be entrusted with a mission.

How calm the sea had been: as if the waters had been charmed by the Halcyon, the fabled bird breeding in its nest floating on the waves; and the dove of white marble gave herself to the breeze which carried her over the island of Crete. Then she swooped down towards the land where Zeus, father of the Olympians, had been born and doves had fed the god with honey. But in the island of terracotta beehives, where a priest king walked amidst the lilies, the dark blue dolphins dancing on pale blue frescoes had not seen the Lost Dove. So to Hellas she flew, to search for the Lost Dove, the Dove of Peace.

Over Mount Hymettus she glided; a dove of white marble made amethyst by the rays of the sunset glowing deep violet over the mountain, and in the cleft of a rock full of juniper and sweet-smelling herbs, she went to sleep.

The caress of dawn woke her, and the bees which once had sweetened the lips of Plato with Mount Hymettus honey now offered some to the dove. But they had not seen the Lost Dove, the Dove of Peace.

Over the fields of poppies she flew, on to Mount Helicon, where bushes of wild strawberries grow. This was the home of the Muses, who had given to Ancient Greece music and the inspiration of poetry – which Hellas, made luminous by the beauty of the voice in her soul, would in time give in her turn to humanity.

That night, the dove rested by the sepulchre of Orpheus, the poet musician who, taught by the Muses, had enchanted man and beast with the strains of his lyre, and charmed the rocks and the trees with the sound of his music. The air was scented with thyme and lavender, and she heard the nightingales' song – some say that the nightingales which build their nests near Orpheus' sepulchre sing sweeter than nightingales anywhere else in the world – but the nightingales had not seen the Lost Dove, the Dove of Peace.

So she flew on to Olympia, where one night, while she was resting in a wild olive tree, an owl – the bird of wisdom – appeared. 'I am looking for the Lost Dove, the Dove of Peace,' said the dove of white marble, her wings amidst the silver leaves touched by shards of moonlight.

All throughout the night, the owl spoke while the moon bathed the ancient stadium and the ruins of the once sacred city where Olympism was born with the magic of her light. Some say that it was Heracles – guardian of the cradle of Zeus in Crete – who had brought the wild olive to Olympia when the hero's brothers ran a race there; he crowned the winner with the leaves which chase away evil spirits. So started the Games in ancient times.

'Later, from throughout the Greek world, when sport had become an integral part of the Ancient Greek's education,' the owl continued, 'athletes came to Olympia. Under the protection of the gods, every four years they came to compete in

Games held in a spirit of fair play and mutual respect, friendship and peace. Then sport was at its noblest – when the body in all its physical power and beauty, and the mind of man, were in true harmony.'

In the scented night, the moon shone over the waters of Alpheios, the hunter who in a golden age, for the love of a nymph, had become a river; its waters so loved by Zeus that the god had placed his most sacred sanctuary among the groves of Olympia. Now the owl continued: 'As the start of the Games approached, Olympia would send ambassadors to the city states of the Greek world, to call and announce the sacred truce, the Olympic Truce Pledge which the Ancient Greeks called *Ekecheiria*; during which all hostilities were suspended and they could safely travel throughout the Hellenic world.

'The ancient Greeks hated Ares, the god of war. They marked the site of a victory by a plain wooden pole on which was placed a suit of captured

armour. When the trophy fell to pieces, the law forbade them to repair it. "It would be invidious and malignant," Plutarch had written, "that we men should ourselves repair and renew the monuments of hatred towards our enemies, when Time himself is making them dim."'

By the morning, the owl had flown away. Accompanied by the song of the cicadas, the dove of white marble left Olympia to bring back to man the ancient Olympic Spirit and *Ekecheiria*, the holding back of the hand ready to strike; hands brought together by the Olympic Spirit, to be joined in friendship and in brotherhood when the barriers between races and creeds are broken, and the memory of old enmities forgotten. 'Of all the gifts that wisdom provides for our happiness, the gift of friendship is by far the greatest,' Epicure, the Athenian philosopher, had said.

A garland of wild olive leaves round her neck, the dove of white marble was flying home. But first

she flew to the mimosa grove to tell her tale,
enfolded by the elusive blue of hope . . .

Now it was summer in the village, when fields of
corn and maize gently sway in their abundance
under the caress of a hazy breeze; when grapes get
drunk with sunshine; and lizards stretch lazily on
the stone.

In the shade of the pear tree from which a
long time ago his grandfather had engraved the
dove, Stefan sat while she told another tale . . .

V

A DOVE PAINTED BY GIOTTO
WHICH FLEW TO THE LAND
OF THE GREAT PLAINS

This we know
the earth does not belong to man;
man belongs to the earth. This we know.
All things are connected, like the blood
which unites one family. All things are connected.
Whatever befalls the earth befalls
the sons of the earth.
Man did not weave the web of life, he is merely
a strand in it.
Whatever he does to the web, he does to himself.

Chief Seattle

For centuries in the hills of Umbria she had been listening to Saint Francis singing with nature and all of God's creatures. But when summoned to the Council on the Mount of Olives, the dove born under the brush of Giotto had left her fresco and flown to the Land of the Great Plains to search for the Lost Dove, the Dove of Peace.

In the Land of the Great Plains the dove met a snowy owl who had once heard Fools Crow say that 'the power and ways are given to us to be passed on to others, and to think or do anything else is pure selfishness. We only keep them and get more by giving them away, and if we do not, we lose them.'

She had flown to the Land of the Great Plains where all comes from *Wakan Tanka*, the One Above, the Great Spirit who made everything in the form of a circle, and all are children of one mother.

For many moons, in the Land of the Great Plains where elk and bison once ran, the dove sat on the branch of a pine tree next to the snowy owl, listening to his words of wisdom – the old Indian wisdom of men and women who loved, respected, and protected Mother Earth; and with the spring came the red dragonfly, sprouting wings; and with the summer the yellow dragonfly, skimming across the waters, seeking and growing. Then one day the snowy owl spoke the words of Chief Standing Bear.

'The Lakota was a lover of nature . . . the old Lakota was wise. He knew that man's heart, away from nature, becomes hard; he knew that lack of respect for growing, living things soon led to lack of respect for humans too. So he kept his youth close to its softening influence . . . Sitting on the ground meditating on life and its meaning, accepting the kinship of all creatures and acknowledging unity with the universe of things, he was infusing into his being the true essence of civilization.'

With the autumn the blue dragonfly had come and gone, and soon the winter dragonfly would go to sleep under the snow – 'the white snow which cleanses Mother Earth,' explained the snowy owl, 'putting her to sleep so that she can gather strength to prepare and create the beauty of spring.'

Now the owl paused. 'But have you seen the Lost Dove, the Dove of Peace?' asked the Assisi dove. So the snowy owl, who once had listened to Fools Crow, told her of Black Elk's vision, which, before he passed away, Black Elk, the holy man of the Oglala Sioux, had told to the white man John Niehardt

whom he had adopted as Flaming Rainbow.

Black Elk's vision taught that Peace is born within the souls of men when they realize their relationship and their oneness with the universe and all its powers. Taken on a cloud to a great plain by two men with flaming spears, Black Elk (who then was nine years old) was welcomed by a bay horse. And to the rainbow-covered lodge of the Six Powers of the Universe – encompassing the four directions, Mother Earth and Father Sky – Black Elk walked with the bay horse, followed by black, white, sorrel and buckskin horses that marched four by four.

The First Grandfather, the power of the west, spoke to Black Elk of understanding, and with flames of many colours the rainbow leapt over him. He gave Black Elk a wooden cup full of living water, and the sacred bow; the power to make live and the power to destroy.

The Second Grandfather, the power of the north, gave Black Elk a white wing and the healing sage herb that grows where the white giant lives; the power to cleanse and the power to heal.

The Third Grandfather, the power of the red dawn which rises in the east, gave him the sacred pipe – the power of peace. Then the Fourth Grandfather, the power of the south, gave Black Elk a flowering red stick and said, 'It shall stand in the centre of the nation's circle. A cane to walk with and a people's heart, and by your power you shall make it blossom.'

The Fifth Grandfather, the Spirit of the Sky, became an eagle and told Black Elk that all things of the sky – the wings, the winds and the stars – would be as relatives and would offer their help. And the Sixth Grandfather, who was the Spirit of the Earth, said, 'My boy, have courage, for my power shall be yours, and you shall need it. Come . . .'

'I started riding,' said Black Elk, 'and I saw that the earth was now silent in a sick green light, and I saw the hills look up, afraid, and the grasses on the hills and all the animals. Everywhere about me were the cries of frightened birds and the sound of fleeing wings. Flames were rising from the waters and in the flames a blue man lived. The dust was floating all about him in the air, the grass was short and withered, the trees were wilting, two-legged and four-legged beings lay there thin and panting and wings too weak to fly.'

'But then,' continued the snowy owl, 'the Grandfathers called on Black Elk, to whom they had given knowledge and wisdom, and with the sacred bow Black Elk destroyed the blue man, he who represented man's greed and abuse of Mother Earth.

'Then a voice said, "Behold, they have given you the centre of the nation's hoop to make it live. Give them now the flowering stick that they may flourish, and the sacred pipe that they may know the power that is Peace, and the wing of the white giant that they may have endurance and face all winds with courage."

'Black Elk took the red stick and thrust it into the earth. As it touched the earth, it became a rustling tree, a cottonwood, very tall and full of leafy branches, and beneath it all the animals were mingling with the people and making happy cries ... But then the people broke camp again ... each seemed to have their own little vision, followed their own rules ... and all over the universe, Black Elk could hear the winds at war like wild beasts fighting.

'Black Elk wept,' said the snowy owl. 'Then he saw a sacred man who was painted red all over his body ... When he got up it was a fat bison standing there and where the bison stood a sacred herb sprang up right where the tree had been, in the centre of the nation's hoop. The herb grew and bore four blossoms on a single stem – blue, white, scarlet, and yellow ... Then the voice said, "Behold this day, for it is yours to make."

'"I looked ahead," said Black Elk, "and saw the mountains there with rocks and forests on them, and from the mountains flashed all colours upwards to the heavens. Then I was standing on the highest mountain of them all and round about beneath me was the whole hoop of the world. And while I stood there I saw more than I can tell and I understood more than I saw; for I was seeing in a sacred manner the shapes of all things in the spirit, and the shape of all shapes as they must live together like one being. And I saw that the sacred hoop of my people was one of many hoops that made one circle, wide as daylight and as starlight, and in the centre grew one mighty flowering tree to shelter all the children of one mother and one father. And I saw that it was holy.

'"Then as I stood there, two men were coming from the east, head first like arrows flying, and between them rose the daybreak star. They came and gave a herb to me and said, 'With this on earth you shall undertake anything and do it.' It was the daybreak-star herb, the herb of understanding, and they told me to drop it on the earth. I saw it falling far, and when it struck the earth, it rooted and grew and flowered, four blossoms on one stem; and the rays from these streamed upwards to the heavens so that all creatures saw it and in no place was there darkness."

'Such was the vision of Black Elk,' said the snowy owl to the dove. 'But shortly before he died, believing that his vision had failed, Black Elk climbed and stood on top of Harney Peak, pleading with the Grandfathers. "It may be that some little root of the sacred tree still lives," Black Elk cried out. "Nourish it then, that it may leaf and bloom and be filled with singing birds."

The dove had then left the Land of the Great Plains. It was the hour when in the east the sun is rising. On the ground, acknowledging the new day which brings new knowledge and wisdom, a man whose heart was pure was beseeching the four directions. *Awanyanka Ina Maka* – Mother Earth, I seek to protect you, he chanted. And the man whose heart was pure followed the flight of the dove returning home. The dove that carried a root of the daybreak-star herb, the herb of understanding, for man and woman to make it bloom.

But first she flew to the mimosa grove to tell her tale, enfolded by the elusive blue of hope . . .

The *vendanges*, the glorious harvest of grapes bursting with juice, had come to the village. And Stefan's dove had many more tales to tell . . .

CHAPTER

VI

A DOVE PAINTED BY
BRAQUE WHICH FLEW TO
THE LAND OF FRESH RICE
EARS OF A THOUSAND
AUTUMNS

Thoughts arise endlessly,
There is a span to every life.
One hundred years, thirty-six thousand
   days
The spring through, the butterfly dreams

Daichi

*T*he brush of an inspired artist had placed her on
the Etruscan Ceiling in the Louvre Museum. But
the dove painted by Braque, whose wings had sailed
the purity of the blue space and borne aloft the
dreams of the visitors gazing upwards at the Ceiling,
had one day received a call from the Council of
Doves . . . and to the Land of Japan she had flown,
to search for the Lost Dove, the Dove of Peace.

The heart of the dove was sorrowful. She had flown
over the young green rice seedlings to temples
where, tempted by rice offerings, birds had made
their home. Her wings fluttering in the fragrance of

the incense, she asked if they had seen the Lost Dove, the Dove of Peace? But none had seen her.

She had flown to Karuizawa; to its forests of green *motsu*, of wild, delicate pink and red azaleas, to the enchantment of its thousand and one birdsongs, but when she asked the birds if they had seen the Lost Dove, the Dove of Peace, none had seen her.

To waterfalls bathing in the moonlight she had flown. In the pure cool watersprings brought forth by the staff of the Great Master Kobo Daishi – he who harmoniously wove the way of Buddha to Shinto, the venerable ancient way of the gods – she had looked, but she had not found the Lost Dove, and her heart felt heavy. And yet, the cherry trees were about to blossom . . .

Under cherry trees there are no strangers, a poet once wrote. But that was long ago when in the worshippers' heart welled infinite gratitude to the gods of the land, the creators of beauty and wonder throughout the seasons. Now man and nature had become estranged.

In the gentle sadness of dusk, the dove had gone to sleep in an ancient gingko grove. The indigo night, made bronze by the sound of a bell coming from a nearby temple, slowly faded into dawn.

The dove awoke. A man was standing next to her. 'I am searching for the Lost Dove, the Dove of Peace,' she said. The man, who was a Tea Master, bowed in silence and invited the dove to follow him through a weathered, unpainted gate, along the *Roji* – the Dewy Path.

Each stepping stone amidst the thick green moss had been splashed with cooling water, and among the shrubs and trees the dove followed the slow pace of the Tea Master. She was following the same simple pathway on which centuries ago the Grand Tea Master Sen Rikyu had invited his guests to approach the Tea Hut in perfect serenity, discarding the mundane, material world.

Near the entrance of the Tea Hut stood a stone lantern, its light softened by the overhanging branch of a tree; and in a low stone basin, from which the guests in an act of purification washed their hands and rinsed their mouths, water was falling drop by drop, 'washing the dust of one's mind'. Then, stooping low in humility, leaving behind ranks, classes and wealth, the guests entered the Tea Hut, through a small doorway, to share in simplicity and quiet friendship the spirit of *Chado*, the Way of Tea.

The Tea Masters say that through serving and receiving a bowl of tea with gratitude, *Chado* teaches a way of life. Long ago, Sen Rikyu had given in a few simple words the rules of *Chado*. 'Lay the charcoal so that the water boils properly; make the tea to bring out the proper taste; arrange the flowers as they grow in the field; in summer suggest coolness, in winter, warmth; do everything ahead of time; prepare for rain; and give those with whom you find yourself every consideration.'

So in reverence, down the ages, the Tea Masters had given their whole being to the preparation of the Tea-gathering, creating a world of harmony, respect, purity and tranquillity, at one with nature; and, sensitive to the spiritual essence which surrounded them, the guests, freed from material attachments, responded with their hearts, their spirits, and their minds. They would carry this response outside the Tea Hut, into their everyday lives.

In the alcove of the Tea Room hung a calligraphic scroll, with words of enlightenment written by a Zen Master. In a bamboo flower vase a single plum blossom had opened, soft dusted by dew. 'Flowers of hill or dale, put them in a simple vase full or brimming over,' had written Sen Rikyu, 'but when you are arranging them, you must slip your heart in too.'

Quietly, the dove waited. There was incense burning; the fragrance of white sandalwood, gentle, pervasive. The utensils had been cleared and purified. In the hearth a charcoal fire had been lit over a bed of fine ash; the kettle over the fire filled with water from the well to make the tea. Subdued by bamboo shades, the light was soft, restful.

And so it was that on that day, the Tea Master with the dove who was searching for the Lost Dove, the Dove of Peace, shared the peacefulness of a bowl of tea.

Out of a black, rough-textured bowl, the dove drank the thick green tea which reflected in its depths nature's peace, balance and harmony, forever flowing throughout the ever-passing, ever-recreated seasons.

Later she heard a lute played nearby – perhaps the same lute which, 'set in the key of the Fragrant Breeze', was heard by the Lady Sarashina when a thousand years ago she crossed a bridge of dreams in the Golden Age of Genji, the Shining Prince . . .

The dove now flew home, her wings made pearl by

the cherry trees in blossom. She was carrying a small green leaf to remind man of the spirit of *Chado*, when man and woman become one with each other in a heart-to-heart meeting. But first she flew to the mimosa grove to tell her tale, enfolded by the elusive blue of hope . . .

The first snow had fallen, a pure white eiderdown which softly enfolded the village in quiet peace. Birds were flying low, tracing hieroglyphs as they landed on the snow. The fountains which, throughout the year, had told stories of the mountains where their waters were born, were frozen now into translucent silence, but Stefan's dove continued her magic tale . . .

CHAPTER

VII

AN ENCHANTED DOVE
MENTIONED IN THE EARLY
CHRONICLE OF THE IRISH
SAINTS, THE FÉILIRE NA
NAOMH EIREANNACH,
WHICH FLEW TO IONA

*Make peace with yourself, and heaven
and earth will make peace with you. Endeavour
to enter your own inner cell, and you will see the
heavens; because the one and the other are one
and the same, and when you enter one you see the
two.*

Isaak of Syria, the Desert Father

She came from ancient Ireland where once they told the story of Mochaoi, the Abbot of n-Aondruim in Uladh, who, one day as he was cutting wattles to build his church, heard a bird singing on a blackthorn. 'I am come here by command to entertain you with my singing because of the love in your heart,' said the bird, who was an angel. And such was the beauty and the sweetness of the song, continues the Chronicler, that Mochaoi heard it for three hundred years; although to him it felt like an hour. Under the spell of beauty, Mochaoi did not age. Nor did a dove resting on a fir tree nearby – a dove dusted with misty grey, which, centuries later, would be summoned to the Land of the Bible, to a Council of Doves held on the Mount of Olives.

She had flown to the Land of the Bible, where it is said that when God had finished making the world, an angel told Him that nearly all was perfect. One thing only was lacking – speech with which to praise God and His Creation. So God, mingling dust from the four corners of the earth, had fashioned man, breathing a soul unto him. And on the eve of the Sabbath, in the twilight of the sixth day, He created writing and the tools of writing.

Then, from the four corners of the earth, the voices of the scribes rose in answer to the admonishment of Peter, the Abbot of Cluny, who would not be born for centuries yet. *Let the pages be sown with divine letters. Let the seeds of the Word of God be sown on paper which, when ripe – that is when the books are finished – may fill the hungry reader with manifold fruit and appease the longing after heavenly bread . . . Thus truly shall you become a silent preacher of the Word of God, and though your tongue be silent, your hand shall sound in the ear of many nations with a loud voice.*

And the voice of the hymn writer Meir Ben Isaac Nehorai answered: *Could we with ink the ocean fill, were every blade of grass a quill, were the world of parchment made, and every man a scribe by trade, to write the love of God above would drain that ocean dry; nor would the scroll contain the whole, though stretched from sky to sky.*

'I will fly to Iona to search for the Lost Dove, the Dove of Peace,' said the dove. And she left the Land of the Bible (where the Hebrew word Iona means a dove) and flew to the ancient island where Scots and Norse kings and the Lords of the Isles sleep of their last sleep; their dreams lulled by waves which, breaking on sands made blue by cerulean skies, have washed away the footsteps of the Picts, the Gaels, and the Vikings.

Evening was falling as she flew over the Sound. The softness of the light had tinted the skies; and, spreading a mantle of Peace over the opal waters, the fallen rays of the sun had traced a pathway of white shimmering gold. Caught in the web of light, for an infinite moment, the dove lost herself.

On the skerries, the muffled barking of the seals was heard, answering the crying of the gulls. In winter, their loud roaring announced the gales; then the islanders on the shore joined their voices to the sound of the waves, and prayed to the moon, asking the guiding lamp of the ocean to watch over the seafarers.

In the courtyard of the abbey, white doves were cooing. Once grey-pearl and mute – says an ancient Gaelic legend – the doves had looked into the heart of Jesus, who wanted to send Peace to the ends of the world, and their plumage had turned to the purest white; while from their throats for ever would come a soft, drowsy murmur, the voice of Peace.

'Have you seen the Lost Dove, the Dove of Peace?' asked the dove of misty grey. In the night rose a haunting melody, *An I mo chridhe, I mo ghràidh* . . . and the doves echoed the Gaelic song *Iona that is my heart's desire, Iona that is my love.*

'But have you seen the Lost Dove, the Dove of Peace?' she asked again.

'There is a hidden pool, a wellspring of Peace,' the doves answered, 'whose waters must be touched at the moment the first rays of the sun awaken them. Perhaps there you will find the Lost Dove.'

At dawn the next day, they accompanied the dove. Her wings brushing the healing waters, she looked into the wellspring. Images of the past came rushing to the surface . . .

She saw the coracle in which centuries ago Columba had left Ireland with twelve of his companions, to sail to Iona, the Gaelic Island of Dreams he would make a fount of learning and of faith.

Now she was flying over the oak church of the monastery, over the cells of wood and wattles. She heard the voices of the monks: *Cantemus in omni die ... in two fold chorus from side to side ... so that the voice strikes every ear with alternating praise .* .. The beauty of the plainchant rose and fell like the waves of the sea, the indigo Sea of Iona with its hues of translucent amethyst and milky jade.

She flew over the library, where precious manuscripts were kept in embossed leather satchels hanging by long straps upon the wall. Then she entered the cell of the Abbot Dorbbene, who was transcribing on vellum *The Life of Columba*, written by the previous Abbot Adomnan after the death of Columcille.

'God be with you,' said the monk.

'I am looking for the Lost Dove, the Dove of Peace,' she said. She tore off one of her feathers which she offered to the monk. With a smile he took the feather (never before had he used a dove's

feather), soaked it until it became soft, and then hardened it in hot sand.

For many days the dove watched the monk writing. His concentration was so intense that the walls of the cell had disappeared; and Time was no more. His breathing had slowed down, to reach in the depths of himself the inner peace through which scribes of all times create beauty.

In the long ago of dreams, an angel had appeared to the Celtic scribe. (Was he the same angel who one day would sit on a blackthorn singing a song of beauty which would be heard for centuries? Who can tell . . .) While the scribe dreamt, the angel gave him designs to memorize, and copy when he awoke. And on the pages of the manuscripts, the scribes of Iona steeped in their Celtic past, 'their work not of men but of angels', were penning the Word of God and the Chronicle of their time in an art of total dedication, awakening our consciousness of the written word.

Then one evening, by the light of the oil, the monk dipped a quill into the ink-horn to write the colophon at the end of the manuscript. As was the custom of the Irish scribes, he asked for the prayers of his readers: *Whosoever reads these books of the miracles of Columba, let him pray to God for me, Dorbbene, that after death I may possess eternal life.* (His manuscript, brought by a monk perhaps fleeing the Vikings and who, like many other Irish monks, went to found monasteries in distant places, would one day find its way to the land where lies the village with the green shutters.)

The dove flew away on her long journey home, enfolded by the elusive blue of hope. But first she flew to the mimosa grove, to tell her tale . . .

In the workshop, Stefan finished writing in the Chronicle. He wondered if the last lines of Dorbbene's manuscript — still glowing today with the same freshness as when written on the Isle of Iona centuries ago – had been transcribed with the quill made of a dove's feather . . . the dove who for centuries sat on a fir tree listening to a song of beauty; who watched Columcille on Iona penning the Psalter, monks illuminating the Gospels, and beginning the Book of Kells.

And still she sits, the dove dusted with misty grey, listening to a song of beauty while we, no longer still and quiet, have forgotten how to let ourselves be. Still she sits, as these manuscripts in the stillness and the spaciousness of each letter, the harmony of their proportions and the singing of their jewelled illuminations, carry to us across the ages the inner peace of their creators – men who created beauty as, their spirit unbounded, they journeyed to their heart.

The skies were low, the village shrouded in mist,

but inside the workshop it was warm. The old stove which, forgotten in the corner, had dozed in silence throughout the summer months, now purred with contentment as Stefan sat with the dove on a bench, warming his hands against the stove's green tiles.

Stefan opened the ancient family Bible from which his grandfather had often read to him. He had been a child then, and from the pear-tree wood-engraving the dove also had listened to the stories of the Bible. Did she know then that she would fly one day to the land of wheat and barley, vine and fig trees and pomegranates; the land of olive trees flowing with milk and honey?

'Tell me what happened to the dove which guided you from the mimosa grove to the Mount of Olives,' Stefan asked her.

The dove went on with the tale . . .